The Case of the Lean Mean Dirt Machine

Adapted by Craig Strasshofer

Based on an original TV episode written and created by Tom Snyder, Bill Braudis, and David Dockterman

Illustrated by Bob Thibeault and Kristine Koob

Adapted by Craig Strasshofer
from an original television show written and created by
Tom Snyder
Bill Braudis
David Dockterman
Produced by Tom Snyder Productions, Inc.

Published by Troll Communications L.L.C.

Created by Kent Publishing Services, Inc.
Designed by Signature Design Group, Inc.

Printed in the United States of America.

10 9 8 7 6 5 4 3 2 1

DUST FIELD DILEMMA

Chloe was a "valley girl," which meant that everything about her was as cool as cool could be. But that was just a hobby. Her job was to be the official tour guide for Gadget Co., Inc., a large company that made many different kinds of big and expensive gadgets. One day, just as she did every Monday through Friday, she stood in front of the main entrance to the company's beautiful world headquarters, surrounded by a small group of tourists. Among the tourists was an inquisitive fellow wearing overalls. Chloe didn't know it, but his name was Eddy.

"Okay, everyone," Chloe began. "Like, welcome to Gadget Co., Inc. My name is Chloe. That's Chloe with a 'CH.' And I'm, like, your tour guide! And we have to stay together through the tour because there's a lot of, like, secret stuff. And it's, like, a secret. So, like, you're not supposed to know about it."

All the people in the group nodded their heads.

"Okay," Chloe continued. "Like, if you will just follow me, we'll begin the tour."

Chloe led the tourists through the tall glass doors and into the building. Soon they were gathered in front of a large window through which they could see lots of big, noisy machines, a series of conveyor belts carrying unfinished gadgets from one place to another, and dozens of workers in orange coveralls scurrying about like busy ants.

Chloe began her official speech. "Okay, this is, like, the part of the factory where a lot of work gets done. Any questions?"

"What are they making now?" a member of the group asked.

"Oh, I don't know," said Chloe, popping her chewing gum. "Any other questions?"

"How much of this is automated?" someone else asked.

"Oh, I don't know," Chloe said with a shrug.

Meanwhile, Eddy was wandering away from the group. Chloe called out to him,

"Uh, sir, can you, like, stay with the group? I'm kind of responsible for everyone's safety."

"I'm safe," said Eddy.

The tour group moved on to a special section of the building that contained the LFI-700. On the door was a sign that read:

TOP-SECRET ROOM

(The Room Isn't Secret, Just the Stuff Inside It)

"And this area is top-secret," said Chloe. "That means the LFI-700 machine that's in here. Like, you're really not supposed to know about it yet. So don't look, okay?" As she spoke, she noticed that strange man, Eddy, flipping through a notebook on a table and peeking into a file cabinet drawer. "Uh, sir," she said, "you, like, really shouldn't be looking in there."

"I'm just curious," Eddy replied.

"Yeah, whatever," Chloe said with a sigh. "Oh, look, we're just in time to see Mayor Daisby present the check for the LFI-700s to the president of Gadget Co., Inc."

"What do the letters L-F-I stand for?" Eddy asked.

"Okay, like, L-F-I stands for Lousy Farmland Improver," said Chloe. "And, like, the 700 stands for, um, the number 700, I guess."

Nearby, a group of reporters, TV camera operators, and spectators had gathered around a platform where Mayor Daisby and Mr. Norton, the president of Gadget Co., Inc., stood. The mayor was holding a huge fake check. Both of them were smiling widely for the cameras. The mayor was just finishing her speech.

"And so," she declared enthusiastically, "Mr. Norton, on behalf of the committee to

AND SO, MR. NORTON, ON BEHALF OF THE COMMITTEE TO FIX UP THE OLD DUST FIELDS . . .

TEN MILLION DOLL

10,000,000

WAIT A MINUTE! WAIT A MINUTE!

fix up the Old Dust Fields . . . "

"Hi, Mayor Daisby," Eddy called out.

"Shush," Chloe hissed.

"Hey, I voted for her," Eddy protested.

"Oh, uh, hello there, sir," the mayor said, trying to be polite.

"My name's Eddy," announced Eddy. "Eddy Watt."

"Eddy what?" the mayor asked.

"Um, Eddy Watt," Eddy replied.

"Oh, Watt," said the mayor.

"Yeah," said Eddy.

"That was great," Mr. Norton broke in impatiently. "But can we please get back to business here?"

"Oh, certainly," said Mayor Daisby. "For ten LFI-700s, at a million dollars apiece, I present you with this check for . . . "

"Ten million dollars!" exclaimed Eddy.

"Yes, that's right," the mayor said.

"Why are you paying ten million

dollars?" asked Eddy. "That's crazy."

"Because," Mr. Norton explained, "my new LFI-700s will fix up the soil in the Old Dust Fields and make them suitable for farming again."

"That's a lot of money, Mayor Daisby," Eddy said. "Can the city really afford it?"

"Well . . ." the mayor began.

"It doesn't matter if it can," Mr. Norton declared firmly. "The city has to do something. Have you ever seen the Old Dust Fields?"

"Seen them?" Eddy laughed. "I eat lunch there. Mayor, I know the Old Dust Fields, and I can sell you my unit, the EW-800, at a dollar apiece. And don't worry, you won't need ten million of them."

"Mayor, this guy's joking," said Mr. Norton. "It's all some kind of a joke."

"It's not a joke," answered Eddy.

"But, Eddy, can your invention do everything the LFI-700 can?" asked the mayor.

"You mean the LFI-900, don't you, Mayor?" Mr. Norton spoke up quickly. "I just remembered we changed the name."

"Oh, okay," said the mayor, "the LFI-900. Eddy, does your EW-800 do the same thing?"

"Yes," Eddy assured her, "exactly the same. Even more. And it's not called the EW-800. I was mistaken. It's called the EW-1000."

That made Mr. Norton mad.

"Well, Eddy," Mayor Daisby asked, "is your invention ready now?"

"I could have everything ready to go in a couple of days," Eddy replied.

"Mayor Daisby," said Mr. Norton, "we have ten LFI-1100s ready for delivery right now."

"But, Mr. Norton, I have to do what's best for the city," Mayor Daisby told him. "I need to have a look at Eddy's idea before I spend all this money."

At that, Mr. Norton seemed like he was ready to explode. "Chloe," he said, trying hard to keep his temper, "why don't you move your group along?"

"Okay, Daddy," Chloe answered. "Oops. I mean, Mr. Norton. Oh, wait. Daddy, may I, like, borrow the car?"

"Chloe, we'll talk later," Mr. Norton said. "Move the group along, please."

Chloe took the group of tourists to see the cafeteria, and the reporters and camera operators sadly went away without a story. Mr. Norton decided to do something about this Eddy person before he caused any more trouble. After all, as he always said when he was being mean, he hadn't become president of Gadget Co., Inc., by being nice.

2

IN EDDY WATT'S WORKSHOP

A few days after Eddy messed up the ceremony at Gadget Co., Inc., he received some important-looking papers in the mail that he didn't understand. So he called Alison Krempel, ace Science Court attorney, and asked for help. She arrived at his workshop,

along with her trusty assistant, Tim. Eddy Watt's workshop held all the usual tools, but it was also full of, well, just plain weird inventions. Alison examined the important-looking papers while Tim fiddled with some of Eddy's strange gizmos.

"Eddy, do you understand what this means?" Alison asked. "Mr. Norton is accusing you of stealing his secret plans for the LFI- . . . Tim, what's it up to now?"

"Twelve hundred," said Tim.

"Right, the LFI-1200," said Alison.

"But that's crazy," Eddy groaned.

"No," Alison corrected, "that's industrial espionage."

"What does this invention do, Eddy?" Tim asked, picking up a small doohickey.

"I don't know yet," Eddy said. "I'm not finished inventing it."

"These are very serious charges, Eddy," Alison continued. "And if you lose, you'll have to pay millions of dollars."

"What!" exclaimed Eddy.

Tim added, "And if you don't have the money, you'll have to work it off at Mr. Norton's business . . . as a tour guide."

"That's crazy," said Eddy. "I don't want to give tours. I'm shy. Besides, I didn't steal the plans for his LFI-1200."

Just then Tim's cellular phone began to beep. He pulled it out, listened intently for a moment, nodded his head, then snapped it shut and put it back in his pocket. "It's the LFI-1500 now," he said.

"Look," Eddy protested, "I'll show you my EW-um . . . 1600, and you'll see that I clearly *didn't* steal the plans."

"Wait, Eddy," Alison said quickly. "You can't show us yet. A court order has been issued by Judge Gwendolyn Stone of Science Court that prohibits you from showing your invention to anyone, even us."

"Why?" Eddy asked.

"Well," Alison explained, "they don't know if you really stole it or not. They're protecting Mr. Norton's rights."

"You won't be able to show it until Judge Stone says it's okay," Tim added.

Eddy frowned. "That's crazy," he said.

"No," Alison said firmly, "that's Science Court."

"Oh, well, then it's not so crazy," Eddy agreed. "But you *do* believe I didn't steal the plans, don't you?"

"Yes, Eddy," Alison told him reassuringly. "We believe you. Now all we have to do is get a jury of your peers to believe you, too."

IS A COURT ORDER WHEN JUDGE STONE TELLS STENOGRAPHER FRED WHAT TO GET HER FOR LUNCH?
NO, TIM. IT'S AN ORDER MADE BY A COURT THAT TELLS A PERSON TO DO SOMETHING OR NOT TO DO SOMETHING.

3

STENOGRAPHER FRED AND THE POTTED PLANT

On the morning of the important trial, Stenographer Fred, the official Science Court stenographer, was sitting on the courthouse steps watering a potted plant with cute little green stems on it when Science Court beat reporter Jen Betters arrived on the scene.

"Come on, my little green friend," Fred said to the plant. "Here's some water. Drink up so you can be big and strong someday like daddy."

"Hi, Fred," Jen declared in her bubbly way. "What do you have there?"

"A new plant," Fred told her.

"Were you talking to it?" Jen asked.

"Oh yes," Fred replied. "I read that some plants respond very well when you talk to them."

Jen, as usual, was somewhat puzzled by Fred. "Really?" she inquired. "That's . . . fascinating. What kind of plant is it?"

"Well, this one's a philodendron," Fred answered, gently patting the plant's little green stems.

"Oh, nice," Jen said.

"Could you say that a little louder?" Fred asked. "I think the encouragement will do it good."

Although she thought Fred's request was more than a bit strange, Jen leaned in closer to the plant and spoke a little louder than usual. "Nice," she said.

"Can't you say something about the leaves?" Fred pressed her.

Jen put her hands on her hips and cocked her head. “Fred,” she protested, “it’s just a plant.”

Horrified, Fred covered the plant with his hands as if he didn’t want it to hear what Jen had said. “Shhh,” he whispered loudly. Then he turned to the plant and murmured, “She didn’t mean it, honest.”

Jen shrugged and then rolled her eyes heavenward. “I’ll see you inside, Fred,” she sighed as she walked up the steps and into the courtroom.

THE DIRT ON DIRT

Inside the courtroom, Alison, Tim, and Eddy sat at one table while Mr. Norton and his attorney, Doug Savage, sat at another. Stenographer Fred was preparing himself to begin recording the proceedings, wiggling his fingers to make sure they were ready to type at top speed. As usual, Micaela was in the front row of the gallery, eagerly watching as the trial began. Beside her sat Mayor Daisby, looking her best in case someone pointed a camera her way. Jen Betters stood by, microphone in hand, waiting for the red light on the TV camera to light up. And then it did.

"Hi!" she began eagerly. "I'm Jen Betters reporting from Science Court, where science is the law and scientific thinking rules. Today we're going to find out all the dirt on soil and the Old Dust Fields. Here comes Judge Stone now."

As the judge entered the courtroom, Fred turned to his plant and said, "All rise and grow for the Honorable Judge Stone."

"Thank you," Judge Stone replied, then added, ". . . what?"

"I was talking to my plant," Fred explained.

"Oh, you have a plant," the judge said.

"Yeah," Fred answered. "I thought I'd keep it on my desk. You know, cheer up the place a bit."

"Well, good idea, Fred," Judge Stone said supportively. "But, you know, you're going to have to water it, give it plenty of sunlight, change the pot when it gets too big, and make sure the soil is always good."

Fred thought about that for a moment and then handed the judge the plant. "You can have it," he told her.

Judge Stone was quite pleased. "Thank you, Fred," she said. Then she addressed the assembled crowd. "Well now, let's get started. First, I want the jury to know that this case is going to be a little different. It is about two inventions that you will not be able to see."

The members of the jury murmured among themselves.

"They're invisible?" one juror asked.

"Cool!" said another.

"But I just got new glasses," yet another remarked.

"No, no, no," Judge Stone said. "They're not invisible. You'll get to see them, but only when the time is right."

The members of the jury were elated at the news. "Yahoo!" they exclaimed.

"Now, Mr. Savage," the judge went on, "you're representing Mr. Norton, correct?"

"Oh yeah, big time," Doug Savage told her.

"Well then, why don't you please start with your opening statement," the judge suggested.

"Sure, thank you," Doug replied. Then he turned to Alison Krempel and teased, "I get to go fi-irst, I get to go fi-irst." Alison tried to ignore him, while Tim stuck out his tongue.

"Mr. Savage . . ." Judge Stone warned.

"Sorry," Doug said sheepishly. Then he focused his attention on the jury. "Ladies and gentlemen of the jury," he began, "we will show that Eddy Watt did, with malice aforethought—little law term there for you, heh, heh, heh . . . "

"Very professional, Doug," Judge Stone remarked.

"Thank you," Doug said proudly. Then he went on, "Eddy Watt sneaked around and stole the secret plans for Mr. Norton's LFI- . . . uh . . ." He leaned close to Mr. Norton and whispered, "What's it up to now?"

"Well, let's see . . . it's a big number," Mr. Norton replied.

"Two thousand?" Doug suggested.

"That's fine," Mr. Norton agreed.

"The LFI-2000," Doug continued. "And we ask that Eddy pay all damages resulting from said theft of said plans, either in said cash or by working as a said tour guide at said company." Doug took a bow and returned to his seat.

"Thank you, Mr. Savage," Judge Stone said. "That was very well done. Ms. Krempel, your opening statement now, please."

Alison Krempel, the attorney for the defense, got up and approached the jury box. "Thank you," she began. "My client loves the

Old Dust Fields. He grew up nearby, played on them as a kid, and now eats his lunch there every day. He cares about them. That's why he came up with his own idea for how to fix the soil so it can be used once again for farming. Eddy Watt didn't steal Mr. Norton's secret plans. He didn't have to, because Eddy already had his own invention—a better and less costly invention. And we'll prove it."

The jury began to mumble, pondering the problem.

"Okay, Mr. Savage." Judge Stone spoke up. "Call your first witness."

"Thank you, Your Honor," Doug said, rising to his feet. "I call Chloe Norton to the stand."

Chloe—valley girl, tour guide, and boss's daughter—took the witness stand. The people in the courtroom could not help but notice how really cool her hair and clothes were. They also saw that her nails looked especially cool—all shiny with silver glitter.

"Hi, Chloe," said Doug, smiling broadly. "Are you nervous?"

"No," Chloe replied.

"Ha, ha, ha," Doug laughed nervously. "I am. Chloe, when was the last time you saw the defendant?"

Chloe glanced at Eddy as if to remind herself. "He was on my tour at Daddy's, I mean, like, Mommy's company, Gadget Co., Inc."

"It's in my wife's name," Mr. Norton muttered. "You know, tax purposes and all."

"Chloe," Doug continued, "did Eddy wander off a lot during the tour?"

"Oh, like, all the time," Chloe replied. "I remember I had to say things like 'Hey, come back here.'"

Dramatically, Doug repeated her phrase. "'Hey . . . come back here.' Hmm. Sounds to me like Eddy had plenty of time to study the secret plans. No further questions. Your witness, Ms. Krempel."

Now Alison approached the witness stand. "Chloe," she said, "approximately how much time would Eddy have had to steal the plans during your tour? One minute? Two minutes?"

"Oh, it was, like, more like sixty," Chloe responded.

"Sixty minutes?" Alison asked firmly. "You mean an hour?"

"I don't know." Chloe frowned. "I didn't figure it out yet."

"Well, no further questions," Alison declared.

Then Doug Savage spoke up. "Your Honor, Chloe is practically an eyewitness. This case is obviously so open and shut that I'm shutting my side of it right now."

"So you're resting your case?" Judge Stone asked.

"Yes," Doug confirmed.

"Okay then." Judge Stone shrugged. "Ms. Krempel, call a witness."

"Thank you, Your Honor," Alison said. "I call Professor Keisha Moss to the stand."

Professor Moss stood up and began to walk slowly toward the witness stand.

"But first," Alison went on, "I'd like permission to move the trial to the Old Dust Fields."

"Good idea. Let's go," said Judge Stone.

The members of the jury thought it was a good idea, too, because it meant they got to go outside.

"All right!" yelled one juror.

"Cool!" shouted another.

"We get to go outside!" added a third.

Judge Stone banged her gavel, declared a recess, and ordered the court to assemble at the Old Dust Fields as soon as possible.

5

LIVE FROM THE OLD DUST FIELDS

A temporary courtroom was quickly set up in the middle of the Old Dust Fields. Judge Stone was at her portable desk. A jury box and two large lawyer tables had been fashioned from used cardboard boxes. The spectators sat on blankets on the ground. It was sort of like a big picnic.

"Okay, Ms. Krempel," Judge Stone said once everyone was in place, "it's all yours."

"Thank you, Your Honor," Alison said. "Now, I call Professor Keisha Moss to the stand."

With that, Professor Keisha Moss took

the witness stand. (Actually, she was only an Assistant Professor.)

"Actually, I'm really only an Assistant Professor," Keisha explained.

"Ah-ha!" exclaimed Doug Savage.

"Ah-ha what?" Alison demanded.

"Don't 'Ah-ha what' me after I just 'Ah-ha-ed' you," Doug protested.

"What?" Judge Stone asked.

"Present," said Eddy Watt.

"I said 'what,' not 'Watt,'" the frustrated judge replied. "Mr. Savage, do you have an objection?"

"To what, Watt?" Doug asked, becoming a bit confused.

"What?" asked Eddy Watt.

Judge Stone banged her gavel so hard her portable desk shook and shimmied. "Okay, that's enough," she said. "Everybody stop it."

Silence fell over the group assembled in the middle of the Old Dust Fields.

"Now then," said Judge Stone, taking a long, deep breath, "Ms. Krempel, question your witness."

"Very well. Ms. Moss," Alison began, "can you please tell us what the problem is with the soil in these fields?"

"Sure," said Keisha. "Any soil suitable for farming needs to have a good mix of organic and inorganic materials. These fields do not."

"Objection," Doug objected. "What do organic and inorganic materials have to do with soil?"

"You really don't know what those words mean, do you, Mr. Savage?" Judge Stone asked Doug in amazement.

"Well . . . no," Doug replied.

Judge Stone then turned to Assistant Professor Moss. "Keisha," she said, "could you please explain 'organic' and 'inorganic' to Mr. Savage?"

"And the word 'ubiquitous,'" Doug added.

"She didn't use the word 'ubiquitous,'" said Judge Stone.

"Yeah," Doug commented, "but I don't know what it means, and I've been hearing it everywhere."

"I'll tell you later," Judge Stone told him. "Continue, Keisha."

"Thanks," Keisha replied. "'Organic' means something's alive, or used to be. In soil it's called 'humus,' which is a mixture of dead plant and animal debris."

"Yuck, that's gross," Doug said. "I call for a mistrial."

"It's not gross," Micaela chimed in. "It's science."

"Thank you," Judge Stone said to Micaela. Then to Keisha she said, "Continue, please."

Keisha went on. "Inorganic material is nonliving stuff, like sand, silt, and clay."

"Can you show us the condition of the soil in these fields?" Alison asked.

SOME FARMERS AND GARDENERS USE LEAVES, GRASS CLIPPINGS, LEFTOVER FOOD, AND OTHER THINGS TO MAKE A MIXTURE CALLED COMPOST, WHICH THEY MIX INTO THEIR SOIL. COMPOST IS RICH IN ORGANIC MATTER, AND THAT MAKES PLANTS GROW BETTER.

"Certainly," Keisha replied confidently. She produced several jars of soil and placed them on a small table that was actually a cardboard box. "I've collected soil in these jars from different parts of the field and from different depths. Now, I'll take three of the jars, fill them with water, shake them up, and wait for them to . . ."

As Keisha spoke, she added water to three of the jars and shook them vigorously. Stenographer Fred dove under his cardboard desk, quaking in fear.

"Are they going to explode?" he asked.

"No," Keisha assured him. "We wait for the soil to settle."

"Your Honor, I object," Doug said. "This experiment is totally . . . ubiquitous."

"You're not using the word correctly, Mr. Savage," Alison scolded.

"So?" Doug replied smugly.

Alison turned to Judge Stone, a look of

frustration on her face. "Your Honor . . . ?"

Judge Stone banged her gavel again. "All right, you two, that's enough," she barked. "I'm going to take a short break and think about the relevance of this demonstration. Science Court is recessed." And with that she gave her gavel another hearty slam.

"All rise," said Stenographer Fred. "All wander around, but don't go too far."

6

THINGS SETTLE DOWN

When the recess was over, everyone returned to the temporary courtroom and sat down. A little gust of wind kicked up a cloud of dust as the trial resumed.

"Science Court is back in session," Stenographer Fred coughed, "but not back in the courtroom." He coughed again. "We're still out here in the Old Dust Fields, in case anyone didn't notice."

"Thank you, Stenographer Fred," said Judge Stone. "Uh, now, I have decided to overrule your objection, Mr. Savage, and allow this demonstration. After all, we have to know what kind of soil we're dealing with. Ms. Krempel, please continue."

"Okay," said Alison. "Keisha, let's have a look at those jars of soil."

Everyone looked carefully to see what had happened inside the jars. The soil had settled, all right, and had formed layers at the bottom of each jar.

"Well," Keisha said, "we can see that the soil is divided into three layers. The bottom layer is sand. Although the particles of sand are small, they can be seen with the naked eye, and they feel rough. The second layer is silt. Silt particles can barely be seen without a microscope, and they feel more like fine flour. The top layer is clay, and these particles are invisible to the naked eye . . ."

"I can see it, and my eye's not wearing anything," Doug interrupted.

"She's talking about the tiny individual particles," Micaela whispered.

THE SAND, SILT, AND CLAY THAT SETTLED OUT OF THE MIXTURE IN THIS JAR ARE CALLED SEDIMENT. UNDER THE RIGHT CONDITIONS, OVER LONG PERIODS OF TIME, THIS MATERIAL CAN TURN INTO SEDIMENTARY ROCK.
CLAY
SILT
SAND

"Oh," said Doug.

"Anyway," Keisha continued, "the clay particles form a gummy mass when wet. All of these particles are inorganic. It's nice to have a good mix of these three types. It helps water move through the soil."

"What about the organic material, the humus?" Alison asked.

Keisha studied the jars closely. "I would have to say, based on these samples, that there doesn't appear to be enough humus spread around at all. It will take a lot of work to get it mixed up properly."

"Mixing these materials up is very important, isn't it?" said Alison.

"Oh, yes, definitely," replied Keisha. "You need something that's going to go through every part of the soil. The main source of nutrients for plant life in soil is decomposing dead plant and animal stuff. The more this is mixed in, the better plants

grow. We refer to this type of soil as 'fertile.'"

"Thank you, Keisha," said Alison. "And that, ladies and gentlemen of the jury, is what my client's EW-3700 does. And it does it better than Mr. Norton's machine. No further questions."

Mr. Norton quickly turned to Doug and whispered, "Hey, why don't you object to that comment? She's putting ideas in their heads."

Doug disagreed. "No, she's not," he said. "She's just saying that Eddy's invention is better than yours."

"Any more questions, Mr. Savage?" Judge Stone asked.

"No, not for this witness," Doug replied. "I call Eddy Watt to the stand."

Eddy took the stand, and Doug began his line of questioning. "Hi ya, Eddy," he said. "Are you nervous?"

"No," Eddy responded.

"Ha, ha, ha," Doug laughed nervously. "I am. So, anyway . . . Eddy, do you think stealing is wrong?"

"Yes, of course," said Eddy.

"What about that time you stole the candy from the corner store?" Doug asked.

"I never stole any candy," Eddy said.

"You never took any candy from the store when you were nine years old? And your parents found out and took you back to the store and made you return it and apologize?"

"No," Eddy insisted.

Doug pulled a chocolate bar from his pocket, carefully tore off the wrapper, and began eating it as he stared at the sky, deep in thought. "Boy," he pondered. "Who could I be thinking of?"

"Earth to Doug Savage, Earth to Doug Savage," called Judge Stone.

"Huh?" said Doug. "Oh, right, thank you. So, Eddy, do you think your machine can find organic stuff in these fields and mix it with the inorganic stuff?"

"Yup," said Eddy.

"Did you know Mr. Norton's machine can do that?" Doug asked.

"I figured as much," Eddy replied.

"Mr. Norton's unit has sensors in the front that detect organic materials. Then it takes those materials and places them into storage tanks," Doug went on knowingly.

Stenographer Fred began drawing on a large drawing board he just happened to have. "Like this?" he asked.

"Yeah," said Doug. "That's good."

"Well," Eddy argued, "mine does that. And when the humus is in the storage area, mine adds chemicals in order to break it down and make it even easier for plants to use."

"Mine does that," said Mr. Norton.

"His does that," echoed Doug.

"And then mine spreads the new organic stuff all throughout the field," Mr. Norton went on.

Stenographer Fred struggled to draw a picture of a spreader on the board. "W-w-w-wait, let me just . . . uuuh . . . okay," he said.

"Mine does that," Eddy shot back. "And mine adds gluey stuff to the soil to keep it from being too crumbly. Plants like that."

"Mine does that," Mr. Norton said.

"His does that," Doug repeated. "And Mr. Norton's unit has strong, durable treads, like the kind you see on a tank, so it can really dig into the dirt."

"Mine has treads to help it dig right into the dirt, too," said Eddy.

Doug gave Eddy his fiercest lawyer look. "Are you sure you didn't steal his secret plans, Eddy? Because they sound exactly the same."

"I didn't steal his plans," Eddy insisted.

Doug pressed the witness harder. "Eddy, let me ask you something. Do you know that the LFI- . . . " He turned to Mr. Norton. "What's the number now?" he asked.

"Um, just say . . . uh, 3500," said Mr. Norton, "but add an SDX!"

"Right!" Doug nodded. Then he turned back to Eddy. "Do you know that the LFI-3500SDX has an onboard computer, which helps it find fuel for its engine? Now that technology alone costs millions of dollars. Does your unit find its own fuel, Mr. Watt?"

Eddy hesitated for a moment, but then he answered, "Uh, yeah. Yeah, it does."

Doug Savage sensed victory within his grasp, like a shark senses a helpless victim. "Of course it does," he declared. "Because you stole Mr. Norton's plans, didn't you?"

Alison Krempel leaped to her feet. "Objection!" she shouted.

YOU KNOW, SHARKS NEVER GROW UP.
I CAN THINK OF A FEW PEOPLE LIKE THAT.
NO, I MEAN THEY'RE FULLY DEVELOPED AND READY TO HUNT FROM THE DAY THEY'RE BORN. THEY NEVER NEED THEIR PARENTS TO TAKE CARE OF THEM.

"No more questions, Your Honor," Doug said smugly. "He's your witness now, Ms. Krempel."

Alison approached the witness stand. "Eddy," she said calmly. "Do you think a machine such as the one Mr. Savage has been describing might have a tendency to break down, especially if it's working in soil all the time?"

". . . It seems like it might," Eddy replied slowly.

"What about your machine?" Alison asked.

"Well, it could break down, but . . ."

"But?" Alison prompted.

"But mine repairs itself," Eddy said.

"What?" Doug cried in disbelief.

"Why . . . why . . . that's crazy!" said Mr. Norton.

"Hey," Eddy exclaimed, "that's my line. You stole that from me! That's crazy!"

Doug Savage couldn't believe what he'd just heard. "Your machines do all that, even repair themselves, and you're selling them for a dollar apiece?" he asked.

"Yup," Eddy confirmed.

Mr. Norton spoke up. "Your Honor, I demand to see Eddy's invention."

"Hey, I thought I was going to make the demand to see it," Doug objected.

"It doesn't matter," Mr. Norton replied.

"Yeah, but I'm the lawyer here," Doug said, pouting. "I mean, I really should be the one demanding things. That's my job. I've waited all week to demand something."

"All right, then," Mr. Norton conceded gruffly, "go ahead, demand."

"Aw, you don't really want me to demand anything. You're just saying that, aren't you?" Doug moped.

At that Mr. Norton blew his stack. "I demand that you demand that Judge Stone

I SHOULD BE THE ONE DEMANDING THINGS. IT'S MY JOB. I'M A LAWYER.
ALL RIGHT, ALL RIGHT! I DEMAND THAT YOU DEMAND THAT JUDGE STONE DEMAND TO SEE EDDY'S INVENTION.

demand to see Eddy's invention!" he bellowed.

Suddenly Doug was all smiles again. "Thank you! Your Honor, I demand to see Eddy's invention."

"You show us your invention first," said Alison.

Tim slowly leaned over and whispered in Alison's ear, "But, Ms. Krempel, what if it happens to look just like Eddy's? The jury will think he really did steal it."

"Don't you worry, Tim," Alison told him confidently. "I think I just figured out what Eddy's machine looks like."

"All right, Ms. Krempel," Doug said. "We'll show you the LFI-3500SDX."

"Uh, 4000SDX . . . L," Mr. Norton corrected.

"Excuse me. I stand corrected," Doug apologized. "The LFI-4000SDXL. And then you have to show us Eddy's EW-. . ."

"EW-4100SDX-ELPS," said Eddy.

“Oooh,” growled Mr. Norton, obviously annoyed.

“Okay,” Judge Stone announced, “we’ll take a short break and head back to the courtroom. When we get there, we’ll unveil both machines.” She banged her gavel twice, loudly. Everyone stood up, shook out their blankets, closed up their picnic baskets, and prepared to go.

7

AS THE WORM TURNS

Soon everyone was gathered back in the courtroom. Just in front of Judge Stone's desk (the one without the wheels), on either side of the room, were two identical wooden boxes. The boxes were big—6 feet tall, 4 feet wide, and 7 feet long. Jen Betters hesitated until the camera's red light came on, then began her report.

"Well, it's the moment we've all been waiting for," she said with excitement. "We finally get to see what these two machines look like. Let's go now to Judge Stone."

"Okay, order in the court," Judge Stone

said. She banged her gavel, and the plant on her desk quivered as if it might topple over. She turned to the plant and said, "Oh, I'm sorry. Did that frighten you?"

"No," said Stenographer Fred.

"Not you, the plant. I thought . . . oh, never mind," said the judge. "Let's just do it. Mr. Savage, please unveil your client's LFI-whatever."

Doug stood up and pointed a remote control unit at one of the big boxes. He pushed a few buttons, and the front panel of the crate slid open. He pushed another button, and the LFI-whatever came rolling out of the crate. The machine crashed into the low wall in front of the gallery, nearly running over Mayor Daisby, who screamed but kept smiling just in case there was a camera pointed her way. The LFI-whatever careened around the courtroom, destroying everything in its path. The members of the jury were prepared to flee for their lives.

"Watch out!" one screamed.

"Here it comes!" cried another.

"Run for it," yelled a third.

Doug Savage frantically pushed more buttons and finally got the huge machine under control.

"Uh, we still need to work out a few kinks," Mr. Norton explained.

Stenographer Fred held up the drawing he'd been working on. "Hey, look," he said. The drawing looked exactly like Mr. Norton's machine, except that it was a different color.

"Very good job, Stenographer Fred," Judge Stone complimented him. "It looks just like it."

"Thank you." Stenographer Fred smiled modestly. "But I'm not quite happy with the color scheme."

Now all eyes turned to the other crate,

I THINK RACING STRIPES WOULD MAKE IT LOOK MORE COOL!

the one holding Eddy's invention.

"Mr. Watt?" said the judge.

"What?" asked Eddy.

"Let's see it," Judge Stone said.

Slowly, Eddy reached into his shirt pocket and withdrew something so small that no one could tell what it was.

"Is that the key?" Doug asked.

"You might say that," Eddy replied.

Eddy unfolded his fingers and held his open hand out for all to see. There, curled up in his palm, was a worm.

Doug Savage screamed with fright. "Ahhh! It's a snake!"

"It's not a snake," Eddy assured him. "It's a worm."

There was a brief moment of stunned silence. Then Doug Savage screamed again. "Ahhh! It's a worm!"

"Stop fooling around, Eddy," Mr. Norton demanded. "Let's see your machine."

"This is it," Eddy said. "It's a worm."

"Where's the machine?" Mr. Norton wanted to know. "Where's all the expensive modern technology?"

"You don't need it," Eddy explained.

Mayor Daisby was very confused. "You don't?" she asked.

"No," Eddy said confidently. "A worm does everything Mr. Norton's machine does, but it does it more cheaply and naturally."

"Harumph. This is . . . preposterous," snorted Mr. Norton.

Doug Savage screamed again and dove under the table. "Ahhh! It's a preposterous!"

Mayor Daisby decided it was time to get to the heart of the matter. "So, Eddy," she said. "Are you telling me that all we need to do is put a whole bunch of earthworms in the Old Dust Fields?"

"Yeah," said Eddy. "I've got a crate full of them."

Alison Krempel rose to her feet. "Your Honor, may I call Professor Parsons to the stand so he can help clear up some of these questions?" she asked.

"Sure," Judge Stone replied. "I'd like to hear from him myself."

8

A FEW WORDS ON WORMS

Professor Parsons, Science Court's resident expert on everything, took the stand. Today he was going to be an expert on worms. "Hello," he said. "How're we doing? What's the dirt?" He laughed and laughed at his own joke.

"Professor . . ." Alison began. Then she had to wait for Professor Parsons to stop laughing.

Finally the cheerful professor settled down. "Gosh, I'm funny," he said. "Okay, I'm ready now."

"Professor," Alison went on, "what can you tell us about earthworms?"

WORMS AREN'T THE ONLY SPINELESS ANIMALS IN THE WORLD. IN FACT, THERE ARE A LOT MORE OF THEM THAN THERE ARE OF US. THE ONLY ANIMALS THAT DO HAVE BACKBONES ARE FISH, AMPHIBIANS, REPTILES, BIRDS, AND MAMMALS.

"So," Professor Parsons said, "you want to know about worms, and right away you think—Parsons . . . old wormy Parsons . . . old wormy, squirmy Parsons." He laughed again as he produced a large diagram of an earthworm. "Well, worms are truly amazing animals. There are approximately a thousand different types of creatures on earth that we affectionately call earthworms. They are invertebrate animals, which means they have no vertebral column, or backbone."

"That doesn't mean they can do the work of a million-dollar machine," Doug interrupted.

"Will you give me just one minute, Mr. Savage?" Professor Parsons asked. "I only just sat down. The seat's not even warm—or 'worm'—yet. Get it?" He laughed once again. "Anyway, worms burrow through the soil, and as they burrow, they swallow large quantities of earth..."

"They eat dirt?" Doug asked in disbelief.

"That's right," Professor Parsons said. "But that earth often contains considerable amounts of organic stuff."

Tim called out to Judge Stone, "Your Honor, may I please help with some additional information?"

"Of course, Tim," Judge Stone replied.

Tim stood up and read from a book on earthworms that he held in his hands. "'Then they store it, break it down, making it easier for plants to use, and deposit it back into the soil.' Plus, they make the soil less crumbly, right?"

"That's right, my little bookworm," Professor Parsons agreed. "Good for you. And another term for depositing is 'casting.'"

"What does that mean?" asked Doug.

"Basically," Professor Parsons said with a chuckle, "it means pooping."

"No more questions," Alison said. "Your witness, Mr. Savage."

Doug approached the witness stand. "Professor," he began, "worms are so small and slow, do you think they actually make a difference?"

"Well," said the professor, "let me give you an idea of the amount of work worms do. Every bit of good soil you see around you has probably passed through an earthworm at some point."

Doug was stumped. "Oh, well . . . uh, no more questions, then," he said.

"Your Honor," Alison piped up, "I'm ready for my closing argument."

"Me too," said Doug.

"Okay," Judge Stone told them. "Mr. Savage, talk to us."

With all the dignity he could pull together, Doug began his closing argument.

"Ladies and gentlemen of the jury," he said. "I used to think worms were nothing more than gross, squirmy, slimy worms. But now I've learned that they do a lot. Maybe they're a little smarter than I thought. Maybe, just maybe, Eddy stole the secret plans, then turned around and gave them to the worms. Did you ever think of that? I did. Eddy is guilty . . . of something. Thank you."

Then it was Alison Krempel's turn to address the court. "Ladies and gentlemen of the jury, Eddy Watt did not steal anything from Mr. Norton," she declared firmly. "Eddy knew there had to be a less expensive, more natural way to revitalize his beloved dust fields. And he knew that worms could do it. Earthworms play an important role in soil ecology. They make soil more fertile by continually loosening and stirring, eating and casting the soil. Soil is more than just a bunch of dirt, after all. It needs the proper mix of organic and inorganic stuff. Worms take the sand, silt, and clay, and mix it up with decaying plant and animal matter and spread it all around for the plants to use."

"You know," Doug said, "all of a sudden I feel like a bowl of spaghetti."

"That's funny." Micaela giggled. "You don't look like one."

"Okay, good job, Ms. Krempel," said Judge Stone. "Now, jury, it's time for you to go and decide if . . ."

"We have already decided," the jury foreperson broke in.

"Hmm. Well," said the judge, "you still have to go into the deciding room and stand around for a minute and come back out."

"Okay," the foreperson agreed.

Doug Savage turned to his client, Mr. Norton. "Call me crazy," he said, "but I think we've got a good chance."

DID YOU KNOW THAT FARMERS NEED TO ROTATE THEIR CROPS TO KEEP THEIR SOIL HEALTHY?
IS THAT LIKE ROTATING YOUR TIRES?
NOT REALLY. DIFFERENT PLANTS USE UP DIFFERENT CHEMICALS IN THE SOIL. PLANTING DIFFERENT CROPS IN THE SAME SOIL HELPS KEEP THE SOIL FROM GETTING WORN OUT.

THE VERDICT

As the jury returned to the jury box, Stenographer Fred stood up and announced in his most authoritative tone, "Here comes the jury. Pretend like you don't know anything."

Doug turned to Mr. Norton again and said, "I really do think we've got an outside shot at winning this thing."

When the jurors had taken their seats, Judge Stone asked for the official verdict.

The foreperson rose to his feet. "Not guilty," he declared.

"Whoa," said Doug. "Have I got egg on my face or what?"

Mr. Norton just sat there fuming.

"Obviously," the foreperson continued, "Eddy could not have stolen the plans from Mr. Norton."

"Thank you, jurors," Judge Stone said. "I agree with your decision."

"We would also just like to add," the foreperson went on, "that in the future we certainly hope Mayor Daisby does a little more research before she almost spends ten million dollars of the taxpayers' money."

"You're absolutely right," Mayor Daisby conceded.

"Okay," said Judge Stone. "Well, that's it. Science Court is adjourned." She gave her gavel a good hard bang. "Oh, sorry," she apologized to the plant. "Did I scare you?"

"That time you did," said Stenographer Fred.

"Not you, the plant. I was talking to the plant," Judge Stone replied.

"Talking to a plant?" Stenographer Fred wondered. "Wow, she's losing it."

When Jen Betters caught up with Doug Savage in the hallway outside the courtroom, he had worms crawling out of all his pockets. There was even one wiggling around on top of his head.

"Mr. Savage, can you tell me what your thoughts are on this case?" Jen asked as she stuck her microphone up to his face.

"Well, I found out that worms are our friends," said Doug. "And they like me."

Just at that moment, Judge Stone was passing by. She paused for a moment and said with a smile, "Mr. Savage, those worms are 'ubiquitous.'"

AM I UBIQUITOUS YET?
NO, MR. SAVAGE. UBIQUITOUS MEANS SOMETHING THAT'S EVERYWHERE ALL THE TIME. AND I'D SAY YOU'RE GOING NOWHERE.
OBSERVE

10
WORMS AT WORK

A few days later, Chloe Norton had a new job—official tour guide at the Old Dust Fields. She was leading the first tour of the new worm-improvement project. Everyone was there, including Mr. Norton, who had become a big worm fan since the trial. There had already been a ceremony at which Mayor Daisby presented Eddy with a check for a lot less than ten million dollars. Passing through the gate to the new Old Dust Fields, the group saw a sign that read:

RELAX, WORMS AT WORK.

YOU KNOW, EDDY'S A PRETTY BRIGHT GUY. I THINK I'LL HIRE HIM TO WORK FOR ME.

"Now," Chloe said, "if you look over here, like, you'll see some worms. And they're, like, really cool. Um, because, like, they really help to fertilize the soil with their, like, poop and stuff."

Professor Parsons, who stood next to Mr. Norton, laughed. "*Poop* . . . I really love that word," he said.

Mr. Norton laughed, too.

And with Chloe in the lead, the group continued on its way across the new Old Dust Fields, as Eddy's worms quietly did their duty, bringing life back to the worn-out soil.

ACTIVITY

Feed Me!

WHAT YOU NEED:

- scissors
- 4 same-sized drinking glasses
- 4 different colors of food coloring
- 3 white flowers, such as carnations

WHAT YOU DO:

Pour a little food coloring into each glass, one color to a glass.

Fill the glasses about halfway with water.

Trim the ends of the flower stems.

Split part of the stem of one flower in half.

Put a flower in each glass of colored water. Arrange the one with the split stem so that each half of the stem goes into a different glass.

Leave the flowers in a warm room. Watch what happens.

WHAT HAPPENS:

Each flower slowly takes on the color of the water in the glass. The flower with the split stem takes on colors from both glasses.

WHAT IT PROVES:

Plants absorb water and other nutrients through their stems and root systems. The process by which this happens is called "capillary action." When plants absorb water and nutrients from the soil, they deplete the amount of water and nutrients left in the soil.

SEND E-MAIL TO YOUR FAVORITE SCIENCE COURT CHARACTERS AT SCIENCECOURT@TEACHTSP.COM. I'LL MAKE SURE YOUR MAIL GETS DELIVERED TO THE RIGHT PERSON.
For more Science Court fun, and to find out how to bring Science Court into your classroom, visit our web site.
www.TeachTSP.com/classroom/SciCourt